KT-154-789

For Mum and Dad,
Woodlouse circus at dawn . . . sleeping in deserts . . .
deciding to be a writer . . .
Thank you for putting up with me and my crazy
ideas for longer than anyone.
xx

WORST. PIRATE. EVER.

PIRATE
Blunderbeard
WORST. PIRATE. EVER.

 AMY SPARKES & BEN CORT

HarperCollins *Children's Books*

Mum

Blackbeard

Blunderbeard

Hooksy

Pirate Pete

MilDred

Uncle Redbeard

Redruth

Captain Chomp

Barber Rossa

First published in Great Britain by HarperCollins *Children's Books* in 2017
HarperCollins *Children's Books* is a division of HarperCollins*Publishers* Ltd,
1 London Bridge Street, London, SE1 9GF

The HarperCollins website address is: www.harpercollins.co.uk

1

Text © Amy Sparkes 2017
Illustrations © Ben Cort 2017

ISBN 978-00-0-820180-7

Amy Sparkes asserts the moral right to be identified as the author of the work.
Ben Cort asserts the moral right to be identified as the illustrator of the work.

Printed and bound in England by Clays Ltd, St Ives plc

MIX
**Paper from
responsible sources**
FSC® C007454

FSC™ is a non-profit international organisation established to promote
the responsible management of the world's forests. Products carrying the
FSC label are independently certified to assure consumers that they come
from forests that are managed to meet the social, economic and
ecological needs of present and future generations,
and other controlled sources.

Find out more about HarperCollins and the environment at
www.harpercollins.co.uk/green

Amy Sparkes is donating a percentage of her royalties to ICP Support, aiming for every ICP baby to be born safely.

Reg. charity no. 1146449
www.icpsupport.org

Dreamed last night that I was chased by goldfish with gigantic false teeth that turned into my mum and ate all my cupcakes. Am a rubbish pirate. ☹ Thank my lucky starfish that nobody knows how rubbish I really am, especially Mum.

She thinks I spent the last year treasure-hunting round the world. (Did try that once. Got lost. Kept it quiet.) Decided NOT to explain that I spent most of it anchored at Port Nibbles by that yummy bakery. She'd be madder than a parrot with a bee in its beak. Couldn't get away

with staying there much longer, so here
I am. Back in Dead Man's Cove with
Mum. Well, five miles out of Dead Man's
Cove. The other pirates won't let me
come any closer. ☹

Last year stank – I wrecked my ship,
the *Flying Doughnut*, when I mistook rocks
for dolphins (could happen to anyone),
set fire to my britches with my fireproof
lantern (why do these things always
happen in front of my stupid brother,
Blackbeard?) and there was that awful
incident with the piranhas in the toilet
(still having nightmares). Yep, last year
was even worse than the awful jellyfish
jelly Mum made for Christmas.

But, as today is the start of a new year, here are my New Year's resolutions:

1. ~~Be the most fearsomest pirate on the seas EVER.~~ ——→ Too hard.

2. ~~Stop biting nails.~~ ——→ Also too hard.

3. Get over fear of fish (and always check inside the toilet before sitting down).

4. Beat my oh-so-brilliant brother Blackbeard at something. Anything. *Please!!!*

5. Invent a brilliant machine to make me rich and famous.

Yeah. Right.

Need to face it: I'm a complete failure.

At least I have Daggers. He's my best friend.

That's it. My life is over.

This came in the post today.

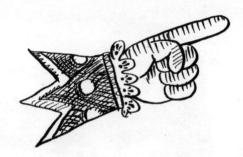

WHAT
AM I
GOING
TO DO?!!!!

Pirates **A**gainst **R**ubbish **P**iracy **S**ociety

The Best Pirate Ship in the World

Dead Man's Cove

The Ocean

January 4th

Dear Barnacles Blunderbeard,

PARPS exists to make sure that only

the finest and rottenest pirates are

allowed to roam the seas. At our recent

Christmas get-together (delicious squid and chips followed by lots of shouting about how rubbish people are) we decided that you are bringing disgrace to the name of pirate. Recent reports of your activities include:

 Fainting at the sight of fish.

Getting lost whilst searching for treasure and asking directions from a tourist in a rubber dinghy.

Failing to credit your account at YoHo Bank with any treasure **<u>AT ALL</u>** over the last year.

Wearing a flowery apron when baking cupcakes.

We regret to inform you that unless one hundred pounds' worth of treasure is credited to your account by the end of the year and, unless your reputation really improves (and you stop wearing that stupid apron), you will be stripped of both the title of pirate and your ship. Any cupcakes found on board will be eaten immediately.

Basically, **YOUR LIFE WILL BE RUINED FOREVER**.

Hope you are well and enjoying the good weather, etc., etc.

Yours sincerely,

Blasterous Blackbeard

(Director of PARPS)

P.S. See you at Mum's birthday party.

P.P.S. And, unless you bring me a really nice cupcake with that scrummy rum-flavoured icing, I'll tell Mum about how much trouble you are in with PARPS.

Just when I thought things couldn't get any worse . . .

I went over to Daggers's cage to give him his daily cupcake, but the cage door was open . . .

Daggers has gone!!!

Found the PARPS letter in the cage, covered with bird poo. Great. So Daggers thinks I'm not a good enough pirate for him. Pirate Pete, who runs the local pet shop, did say Daggers was a smart bird when I bought him.

FINE. JUST FINE.

Life stinks more than Blackbeard's breath.

JANUARY 8TH

To Do List:

~~2pm - Take Daggers to vet for beak rot treatment.~~

TRAITOR!!! MAY ALL YOUR FEATHERS FALL OUT!!!

1. Cancel *Your Parrot* magazine subscription.

2. Send off *Which Pirate Pet?* magazine subscription.

14

3. Find new pirate pet before PARPS find out that Daggers has left.

4. Find a way to get one hundred pounds' worth of treasure and stop myself being banned from the pirating world forever.

5. Finish building Snatch-A-Rat™ machine for Mum's birthday present.

6. Bake nice chocolate cupcake with swirly bits on top to cheer me up.

Finished building the Snatch-A-Rat™
machine. Couple of little problems, but
once I got my thumb free, all was OK.
Mum'll love it. Then maybe she'll see
I'm not a complete waste of space,
whatever Blackbeard says.

Spinny-round arm bit

Rat grabber –
extra-large barbecue tongs

Cheese dispenser
(use Extra Strong Pongwhiff
cheese – yuck!)

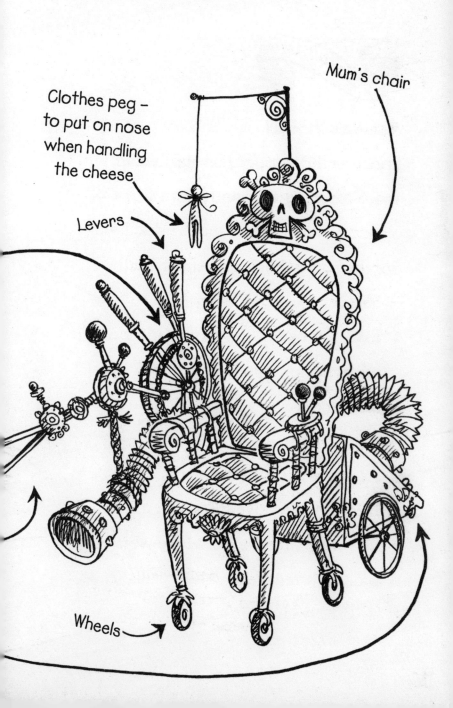

Clothes peg –
to put on nose
when handling
the cheese

Mum's chair

Levers

Wheels

JANUARY 14TH

Mum's birthday!!!

**2pm – Birthday party on Mum's ship,
the *Golden Squid*, Dead Man's Cove.**

So, the party didn't exactly go well:

1. I was late – got my thumb stuck again
   when packing up the Snatch-A-Rat™
   machine.

2. As my rowing boat drew near to
   Dead Man's Cove (the coolest marina
   for pirate ships in the whole world),
   Blackbeard and his mates yelled rude

names at me and pelted me with fish fingers. ☹ **I HATE FISH.**

Even in fingers.

3. In the rush to leave my ship, I forgot the cupcake for Blackbeard. He was furious and told Mum all about the PARPS letter. Then *she* was furious. She said a blindfolded sea cucumber would make a better pirate than me. ☹

I thought the Snatch-A-Rat™ machine would make her happy, then she wouldn't even have to get out of her chair to catch those pesky rats. Turns out, maybe not! Peered closely at the machine to see why my thumb keeps getting stuck. Got my nose stuck. This made the grabber miss the rat and snatch Mum's wig instead. The wig went flying across the boat into her best barrel of rum. Wig + rum = both ruined. Rat = ran off with cheese. Me = in big trouble, with very red nose.

Blackbeard laughed so much his peg leg fell off.

Mum made me walk the plank.

Just before I hit the water, I realised

Blackbeard had hidden my rowing boat! ☹
So I had to swim all the way back to my
ship as quickly as I could with horrible,
yucky fish chasing me all the way. In
the distance, I could hear Mum yelling
that she's entering me for the Pirate of the
Year Award. She knows I'll fail miserably
(Blackbeard always wins, every stupid
year), but she thinks I'll learn a thing or
two about being a proper pirate.

I.

AM.

DOOOOOOOOOMED.

This came in the post.

Pirate of the Year (POTY) Award

Congratulations on entering the POTY Award!

PRIZE: £100 TREASURE

POTY EVENTS:

1) Pirate skills

2) Kraken-wrestling

3) Treasure-hunting on the ISLAND OF DEATH!!!

(Please bring a packed lunch.)

Event One - Pirate Skills: March 1st

Bonus points for *Best Pirate Pet*

Please note:

Meet at Harbour Grudge for each event.

Once you have entered the competition, you can't back out or we'll chase you all over the Seven Seas and call you a wimp.

You will need:

Ship, pirate pet, sharp pointy sword, etc.

Wishing you every success (or at least that you avoid a long and painful death).

Good luck. Let's face it – you'll need it!

Not at all panicking. Not at all panicking.
Not at all panicking. Not at all panicking.

JANUARY 18TH

If I *have* to take part in the POTY
Award, I might as well try not to come
last. Went to Pirate Pete's Pets at Port

Cutlass today to get a new parrot so I can at least be in with a chance of winning Best Pirate Pet. No luck – they were all sold out. Everyone is buying new, fabulous parrots ready for the POTY Award. But Pete said he knew the perfect pet for me and would order it in especially. I've paid up and it's being delivered to the *Flying Doughnut* tomorrow. Pete wouldn't tell me what my pet is. He wants it to be a surprise!

But he told me it's called **BORIS THE BASHER**. Wonder what type of animal it could be? Fearsome feline? Scary sea dog? This will get me more respect in the pirate world.

I hate Pirate Pete.

This is Boris the Basher.

She's a chicken.

Help.

JANUARY 20TH

A *chicken*.

No pirate in the whole history of the world has ever won the POTY Award with a pet *chicken*.

JANUARY 28TH

The stress of the POTY Award has made my hair go all straggly. I need to get a good pirate haircut.

Boris is stressed too. She's lost loads of feathers. And she's got this horrid scaly skin underneath. She looks like an oversized lizard wearing a feather boa.

Will be kicked out of the Pirate Skills event at this rate.

2pm – Hair appointment at Barber Rossa's.
3pm – Feather perm appointment for Boris at Barber Rossa's.

JANUARY 29TH

Never EVER going to Barber Rossa's EVER again.

Before I even looked in the mirror he took a photo to send to *Pirate Life* magazine for their feature on all the POTY Award competitors.

"Oh, great!" I shouted at him when I saw my reflection. "Why don't I just get a princess costume to go with it?"

He just laughed. I hate pirates.

JANUARY 30TH

OK, I REALLY hate pirates.

This arrived in the post today:

To Blunderbeard,

I'm entering the POTY Award.
You have NO CHANCE.
Hahaha.

From,
Barber Rossa

I really don't think my life can get any

worse.

It got worse.

This morning, as I was hanging my washing out on the deck, a cannonball came whizzing through the air. It just missed my head and put a hole right through my favourite jumper on the washing line! I need a safer way to dry my clothes!!

When I went to take a closer look, my heart sank.

Cannonball wrapped in bright pink paper?

Done up with a bow?

Someone wrecking my stuff?

There's only one person who keeps in touch like this. I unwrapped the cannonball and, sure enough, there was a note inside from my dreadful cousin Redruth.

Hey, Blunders!

Great news – I'm entering the POTY Award. Dad thinks I'll win as I've been practising pirating lots: cheating, stealing and generally being nastier than a bite on the bum from a great white shark. He's so proud of me. He reckons I'm such a good pirate that I'll be the one to find the legendary lost treasure horde of Captain Loozer and succeed where every other pirate in the world has failed. Soooooo exciting!

Haven't seen you for ages. Are you still doing those stupid inventions? It'll be great to catch up – can't wait to make you look really, really ridiculous. Though from what Blackbeard's said, you don't need my help with that. He told me about the piranhas in your toilet! Sooooooo funny.

Later, Blunders!

R xxx

Oh, joy.

Spent today on the *Flying Doughnut*, practising for the Pirate Skills event.

Not exactly what you would call a *complete* success.

Cannonball-firing

To help me with my cannonball-firing, I made some little figures to aim at. Decided to model them on Blackbeard – with the hope of blasting them to smithereens . . .

On the plus side, I've invented a game called ten-pin cannonballing. Don't suppose it'll ever catch on.

On the downside, there's
now a hole in my ship.

Plank-balancing

A good pirate can balance on the narrowest
of planks and never fall off.
Fell off.

Rope-climbing

Scared of heights.

Thought a blindfold

might help so

I wouldn't

realise

how high

I was.

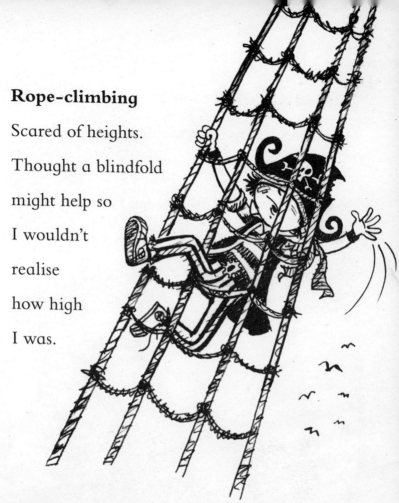

Missed footing as couldn't see where I was

going.

Fell off. Again.

Can no longer sit down.

Sword-fighting

Invented a FowlBlade™ machine to help me train.

Glad to find some use for that hopeless Boris. Added Chick-O-Snack to the mint chocolate cupcakes!

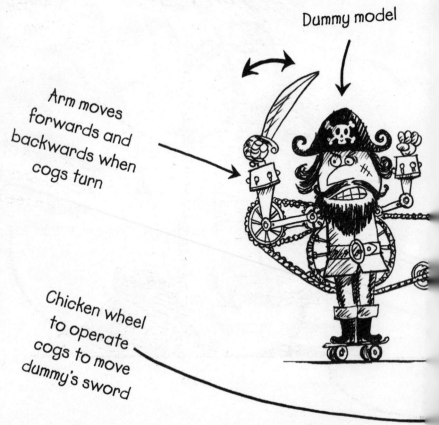

Dummy model

Arm moves forwards and backwards when cogs turn

Chicken wheel to operate cogs to move dummy's sword

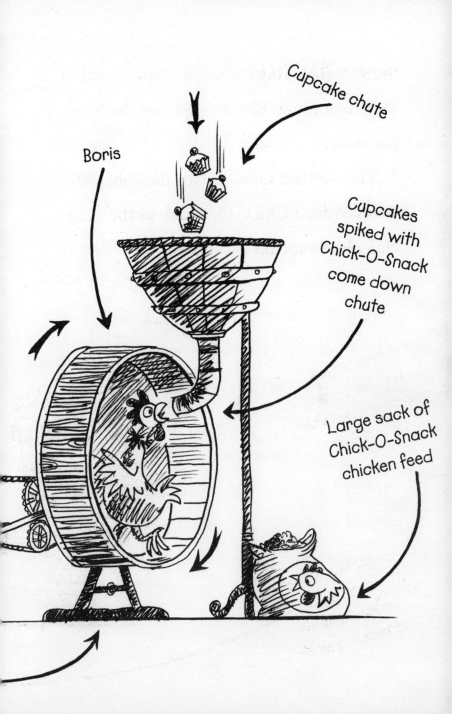

All went well until she'd eaten so many cupcakes she needed to poo and stopped running in the wheel.

The dummy's sword arm whizzed out of control . . .

Took three hours to unpin myself from the cabin wall.

Note to self: in future, line chicken wheel with removable and washable sheets! Took two hours of scrubbing to get all the poo off.

Rewarded myself for all my hard work by eating a cupcake. Accidentally picked up one with Chick-O-Snacks in it! Disgusting!!! Was sick all over chicken wheel.

Another two hours of scrubbing ...

Overall, I think my machine was a great success and I'm delighted with my progress. Not.

FEBRUARY 28TH

Night before the Pirate Skills event.

Cannonball wrapped in bright pink paper smashed through my kitchen porthole and squashed my lemon-and-lime cupcake. ☹ There was another note inside the wrapping:

Hey, Blunders!

See you tomorrow! Last one to Harbour Grudge is a rotten squid! (That'll be you, then.) Guess what? Dad's going to be a POTY judge now. Turns out one of the other judges was mysteriously marooned on a desert island hundreds of miles away so there was a vacancy. Dad offered to step in. Can't wait to make him proud!

Later,
Blunders!

R xxx

Uncle Redbeard a POTY judge?!

Even Blackbeard is scared of him after that incident with the barrel and that humongous lobster. I'm nervous enough about the Pirate Skills event as it is!

Think Boris is nervous too.

Today she laid an egg that looks like this:

Tomorrow I am doomed to failure. And the WHOLE of the pirating world will be turning up to watch.

Better set my alarm clock an hour early to fit in some extra cupcake-eating. That'll cheer me up.

OVERSLEPT!!!!!

Rushed around like mad to get to Harbour Grudge. Forgot Boris. Had to go back, which made me even later.

All the other pirates were laughing at me. Turns out in my rush I forgot to put on my trousers, which Blackbeard kindly pointed

out to the crowd. WITH A MEGAPHONE.
Had to go back to the ship AGAIN!

Usually, not many pirates enter the
POTY Award. Something to do with
the high chance of **COMPLETE AND
UTTER DEATH!!!!!!** But this year
there are lots:

Captain Slasher the Rather Scary,
Redruth, Blackbeard and his mates
Hooksy and MilDred, Barber Rossa . . .

And me.

We all went aboard the POTY ship.
Everyone else was brilliant at Pirate
Skills. Redruth did cartwheels along
the plank and finished with a double
backflip. Her smug little parrot stayed on

her shoulder the whole time. Blackbeard climbed up the rope using only his teeth. Captain Slasher was excellent at sword-fighting. Can see how he got his name . . .

And then it was my turn.

MilDred whispered, "Good luck!" to me when Blackbeard wasn't listening. Reckon I grew two centimetres taller.

I shrugged, looked my coolest and whispered back, "I won't need it." Then I walked smack into the ship's mast.

SMACK. INTO.

Yes, everyone saw. Why does everyone *always* see???? So, with all eyes on me, I took a deep breath and began.

Oh. That. CHICKEN!!

I bet no pirate in the history of the
world has ever had to walk the plank
with a hysterical chicken on their
shoulder. That's because

IT'S
NOT MEANT
TO BE
DONE!!!

Boris hiccupped, which made me wobble . . .

The wobble made her panic and she put her wings over my face . . .

Not being able to see made me wobble even more . . .

Which made Boris squawk hysterically and poo on my nice new hat.

It didn't end well. Though that might have something to do with the fact that Blackbeard stomped on the plank.

Apparently his peg leg "slipped". No more
rum-flavoured
cupcakes for him.
EVER.

And if Boris ever behaves like that again it's chicken nuggets and chips for my tea.

After this dreadful ordeal is over, I'm going to invent a new machine: the ChickPoo-Hurler™, for the next time Blackbeard is a meanie-pants.

Pirate Skills Task Two: Rope-climbing. Climb up the rigging. Ten points for the quickest climber.

Climbed up a bit.

Passed out a bit.

Woke up with a fish on my face.

May have passed out again . . .

Let's move on.

Pirate Skills Task Three: Sword-fighting.
Ten points if you are still standing
after five minutes with Captain
Cutthroat.

The good news? I'm alive.

The bad news? My coat looks like this:

Should really have got my
ten points, but Uncle
Redbeard knocked
off nine of them for
cheating. **Grrrrrr.**
It's not MY fault
I got all mixed up
and thought it was the
cannonball-firing task.

Captain Cutthroat spent four minutes and fifty seconds looking for his hat after my cannonball blasted it off his head. Then he spent the last ten seconds ruining my coat.

The other judges let me keep one point, though. They said cheating showed I had pirate potential after all. Mummy will be pleased. Didn't tell them it wasn't on purpose and that I just got confused. Don't want rude words slashed into my hat too!

Unfortunately, Uncle Redbeard and the other judges chose which rowing boat: mine!

The world hates me.

All in all, I was about as successful as a toothless shark that's lost his false teeth.

The leader board looks like this:

Blackbeard: 30

Captain Slasher the Rather Scary: 29

Barber Rossa: 27

Redruth: 26

MilDred: 20

Hooksy: 19

Me: 1 (and, let's face it, that was by accident)

With my rowing boat sitting at the bottom of the sea, I was a bit stuck. Thankfully, at the end of the day, I found a nice day-tripper with a speedboat and hitched a lift back to the *Flying Doughnut*.

Just as well – didn't want to have to swim
all the way back and look like a complete
idiot. AGAIN.

MARCH 2ND

So this came in the post.

To Blunderbeard,

YOU COMPLETE AND UTTER IDIOT.
PARPS will look forward to taking
over your ship – they need a floating
toilet block for headquarters. Hahaha.

Love (yeah right) from,

Blasterous Blackbeard

(Director of PARPS)

Taking time out from POTY training today to start work on ChickPoo-Hurler™. RIGHT NOW!!! Blackbeard is so smug that he won all the tasks yesterday. He even got extra points for the Best Pirate Pet because his rotten parrot, IronClaw, danced the hornpipe while saying,

"Blunderbeard is an idiot!" in fourteen different languages. Uncle Redbeard laughed so much his glass eye popped out. When I presented Boris to the judges, she stood there looking gormless, farted, laid an egg and walked off.

I give up.

But one day I'll beat Blackbeard at something. **ONE DAY!!!!!**

MARCH 10TH

Final design plan for ChickPoo-Hurler™.

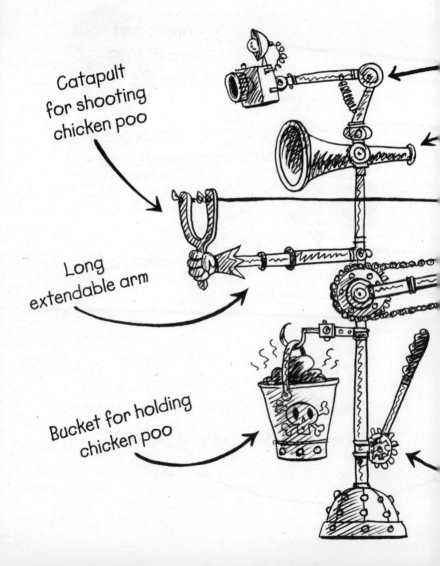

Catapult for shooting chicken poo

Long extendable arm

Bucket for holding chicken poo

REVENGE
SHALL BE MINE!

Separate arm with
camera attached to
capture the moment

Megaphone for announcing how
stupid Blackbeard looks

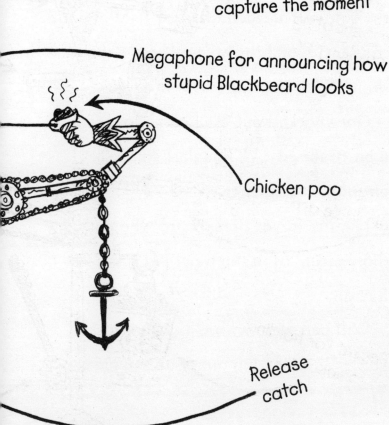

Chicken poo

Release
catch

MARCH 23RD

Few technical hitches with the ChickPoo-Hurler™.

It turns out that it hurts a little bit if the catapult accidentally gets hold of your trousers ... and throws you across the ship ... into the ship's wheel.

Got knocked out. As I came to, I was a bit confused ... Thought I could see piranhas everywhere.

I'm sure it was Blackbeard who put those piranhas in my toilet last year. ☹ Eurrgh.

Will persevere with ChickPoo-Hurler™. Once I'm out of all my plaster.

Hope to recover in time for POTY
Event Two.

Although, after kraken-wrestling, I'll
probably look like this again:

If I survive at all, that is. ☹

I wish Mum hadn't entered me for the POTY Award. But it'd be worth it if I could just win and prove I'm not as useless as she and Blackbeard think.

But how? Because I am . . .

APRIL 10TH

Stress must be getting to Boris. I couldn't find any of my shiny brass buttons this morning.

Turns out she'd been hoarding them all in her bed.

That chicken needs serious help.

APRIL 19TH

Yeek!! This came today. Oh, great. Just great.

Leviathan Cave
Secret Place
The Deep Dark Depths
The Ocean
April 18th

Dear POTY participant,

Congratulations on surviving so far. We hope you have not lost too many limbs/your parrot/ your mind/etc., etc. and that your POTY training is going well.

Event Two – Kraken-wrestling: 10am on July 1st.

Please bring the following with you:

* Diving gear

* Something sharp and pointy

* Packed lunch (light refreshments also available at Pegleg's Pantry)

* Last will and testament

Please note that dynamite is not permitted as the judges of last year's POTY Award are still cleaning kraken out of their beards.

Please read the enclosed kraken fact sheet carefully.

Wishing you good luck, as you will, of course, need it.

Yours sincerely,

Captain Harry Chomp

Senior Officer,
Society for Monsters Existing in Large Lakes and Seas (SMELLS)
(Reg. charity 00000PS)

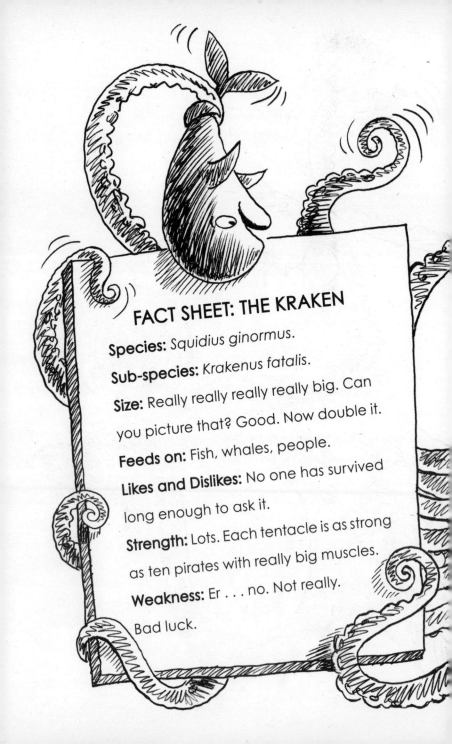

FACT SHEET: THE KRAKEN

Species: *Squidius ginormus.*

Sub-species: *Krakenus fatalis.*

Size: Really really really really big. Can you picture that? Good. Now double it.

Feeds on: Fish, whales, people.

Likes and Dislikes: No one has survived long enough to ask it.

Strength: Lots. Each tentacle is as strong as ten pirates with really big muscles.

Weakness: Er . . . no. Not really. Bad luck.

Perfect.

If I die during this event, I'm leaving Boris to Blackbeard in my will. Serve him right for everything.

APRIL 30TH

Have a secret plan for kraken-wrestling. Will train Boris to scuba dive so she can rescue me.

Minor flaw in said secret plan – I'm struggling to get hold of a scuba diving kit for chickens. Odd.

Pirate Pete at Pirate Pete's Pets says he can make a kit for me. I've paid up and it'll be with me tomorrow. **Excellent!**

At least you stand a chance of beating the kraken. Well, as much chance as you do of finding the legendary treasure hoard of Captain Loozer! You know, the one that every pirate searches for but no one has ever found? Yeah, that one . . . HAHAHA!

Pirate Pete

When this is over, I am going to make Pirate Pete a cupcake filled with bogeys.

This is what he sent me for Boris:

FINE!!!!!!!!

I'll invent my own.

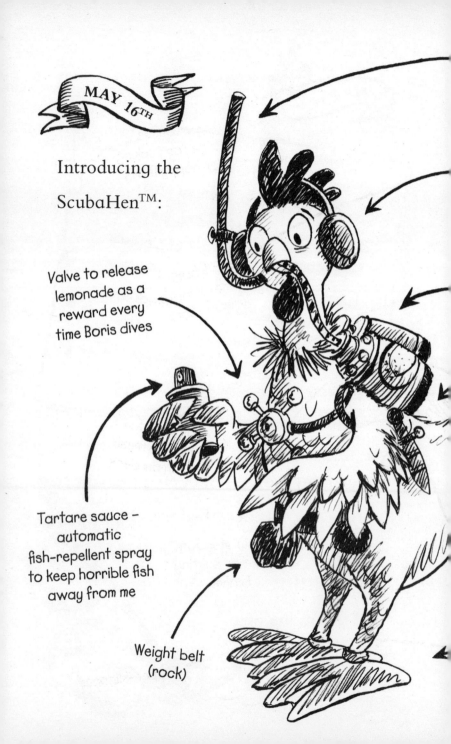

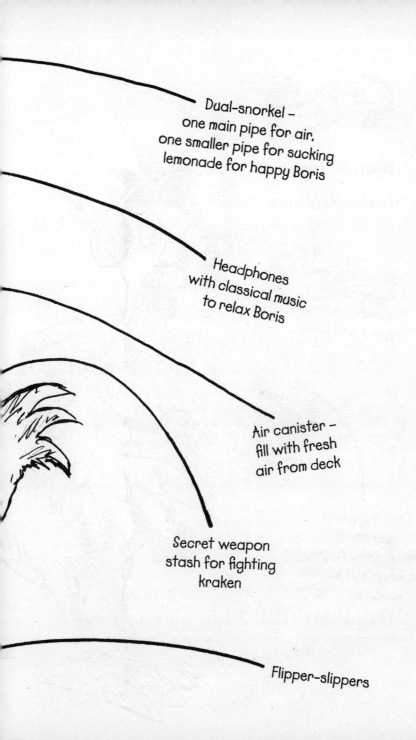

Dual-snorkel –
one main pipe for air,
one smaller pipe for sucking
lemonade for happy Boris

Headphones
with classical music
to relax Boris

Air canister –
fill with fresh
air from deck

Secret weapon
stash for fighting
kraken

Flipper-slippers

MAY 23RD

Boris is a little reluctant to wear the scuba diving kit. Need a plan B.

JUNE 5TH

I cannot think of a plan B.

JUNE 20TH

I STILL cannot think of a plan B.

JUNE 28TH

HELP ME!!!!!! I am going to die

at the tentacles of a kraken!!!!

JUNE 29TH

Aha! I have a plan B: after I've died at
the tentacles of a kraken, come back as
a ghost to haunt Blackbeard and Pirate
Pete.

JUNE 30TH

To whomever finds this diary (you
nosey, rotten . . .). Please make sure
someone reads this speech at my funeral.
Not Blackbeard. He'll make up his
own stuff so I look like a complete
nincompoop.

Here lies to rest Pirate Barnacles Blunderbeard, or what remains of him, after his brave and epic battle with the mighty, fearsome kraken. Let it be said that Barnacles was a remarkable pirate in ~~many ways~~ ~~some ways~~ hmmm. Let it be said that Barnacles was an *unusual* pirate. He may not have been good at walking the plank or getting lots of treasure (oh, if I owe anyone any money – sorry –

buried it somewhere. Forget where.
Ask Blackbeard to pay you back), but he
could bake the best cupcakes this side of
the Bermuda Triangle. And probably the
other side too.

Barnacles was also an unsung
inventing genius. To his beloved brother
Blackbeard, he leaves his nasal-hair
removal machine: the NasoPluck™
and a complimentary roll of bandages.
To Pirate Pete, he leaves his brilliant
AutomaticHelpingHandToiletRoll-
Assistant™ and the phone numbers of an
emergency plumber and doctor. And, to
his dear mother, he leaves his pet chicken,
Boris, in the hope that she might scare

away the rats. Or the rats will scare away
Boris. Either way it's a good outcome.

Farewell, cruel world. Farewell . . .
You stink anyway.

Pirate
Blunderbeard

Event Two – Kraken-wrestling: July 1st.
Up to ten points awarded for
originality, style and survival.

9am – Prepare the last meal of a doomed man: scrambled eggs on toast with black pepper, followed by raspberry cupcake with marshmallows.

10am – Certain death.

Leader board after Event Two:

Blackbeard: 40

Captain Slasher the Rather Scary: 37

Redruth: 35

Barber Rossa: 34

Mildred: 27

Hooksy: 24

Me: 0 ———>They took away my one point. Why? See below. ☹

I'M ALIVE!!! I don't care that Blackbeard won the kraken-wrestling competition (and only because he ended up wrestling an octopus in a bad mood and not a fearsome kraken). The important thing is **I'M ALIVE!!!**

And it's no thanks to that ridiculous chicken Boris. It was my turn to get into the water and I was still trying to wrestle Boris into her ScubaHen™ diving kit. I was terrified and wasn't concentrating so muddled up the pipes. I put the lemonade into the main pipe instead of the air so she took in LOADS of lemonade on the way down! Let's just say Boris doesn't handle sugar rushes very well.

It was bad enough being close to normal fish, but we'd only been in the water a few minutes when the fearsome beast appeared. It was **ABSOLUTELY TERRIFYING**. Had a mouth the size of my rowing boat! The creature started coming towards me. Tentacles waving everywhere. I panicked and decided to swim for it.

Meanwhile, Boris was going mad on a lemonade high, swimming left, right and centre. The kraken got so cross trying to swat her that its tentacles got all tangled up. Boris got past the kraken and swam off in a straight line at a rate of knots.

I lost sight of her.

Then the furious kraken honed in on me. It reached out its only untangled tentacle, grabbed me and turned me upside down.

And that's when it happened.

Turns out, in my state of confusion yesterday morning, I'd mistakenly picked up the pepper pot from the breakfast table instead of my pocket watch. As the kraken turned me upside down, the pepper pot fell out of my pocket and landed on the kraken's face.

See opposite:

Leviathan Cave

Secret Place

The Deep Dark Depths

The Ocean

July 1st

~~Dear~~ Pirate Blunderbeard,

It appears you have discovered that my *Krakenus fatalis* has an allergic reaction to pepper. You might think we'd be grateful for this information, however, there is a slight drawback. THE THING WON'T STOP SNEEZING! It may not have crossed your puny, silly, little mind that a massive sea monster with a massive sniffle causes a MASSIVE problem. Do you know how much trouble I am in for providing a faulty kraken? Do you?

83

That sneezing kraken has now caused thirty-eight shipwrecks, four tidal waves AND is responsible for ice cream being forcefully splattered over Mrs Chomp's new dress. It goes without saying that the kraken is now out of action for the rest of the event. Do you know how hard it is to catch a new kraken? DO YOU?! All I could offer the POTY judges as a replacement was a grumpy octopus, which Blackbeard easily defeated. Everyone is more than slightly miffed with you. The pitiful one point you scored during the first event has been taken away. And you have now been blacklisted from EVERYWHERE. IN THE WORLD.

I'm glad that you were blasted several hundred

metres out of the sea when the kraken sneezed. And I'm glad you landed on the roof of that lighthouse. Teeth first.

Yours angrily,

Captain Harry Chomp

P.S. And keep your stupid chicken away from my creatures. It appears to have left a French plait in my kraken's tentacles. Do you know how hard it is to unplait a kraken? **DO YOU?!**

Whoops. ☹

1. Make an appointment for
   emergency dental treatment at
   Basher's Gnashers.

2. Remove all traces of ScubaHen™
   lemonade from the rowing boat.

3. Pick up Boris from the other side
   of the ocean.

4. Create disguise to hide from Captain Chomp and other angry pirates.

5. Think up another way to get one hundred pounds for PARPS – there's as much chance of me winning this competition now as there is of Blackbeard taking up ballet.

JULY 8TH

Had a rummage on the ship to find a disguise for when I go out later. Came up with this:

10am – Appointment with Old Basher at Basher's Gnashers.

Needed to replace the teeth knocked out by the lighthouse. Of course, I didn't have any gold for gold teeth. All I could find in my pocket was half a packet of jelly beans, so had to have new teeth made from those. Hope they won't give away my disguise. Old Basher nearly died laughing. I really, **REALLY** need to get me some gold. ☹ Shame no one knows where to find the lost treasure

of Captain Loozer. That massive
hoard of gold stolen from the cave
of the dragon Flametongue would be
quite handy right now.

JULY 14TH

Cannonball through the window.

Wrapped in pink paper. Squashed
cupcake.

What does she want *now*?

Hey, Blunders!

Is this you?????? Tell me this isn't you! I haven't laughed so much in ages. Dad sent it to PARPS and showed all the POTY judges. They've said they'll take it into consideration.

Got to dash. Dad's taking me out to practise treasure-hunting. Sooooooo can't wait until Event Three!

Later,

R xxx

I hate my life.

JULY 31ST

WAYS TO GET ONE HUNDRED
POUNDS FOR PARPS:

1. ~~Sell my brilliant genius brain to scientists (slight drawback - will have no brain left).~~

2. ~~Bake giant cupcake and hold a raffle (but other pirates already think I'm lame enough as it is).~~

3. ~~Find legendary hoard of Captain Loozer (impossible as it probably doesn't exist).~~

4. ~~Ask Blackbeard to loan me some cash because he's my big brother (yeah ... that's funny).~~

5. Win POTY Award.

Drat.

AUGUST 11TH

Boris has had hiccups ever since the kraken-wrestling incident. The lemonade from the ScubaHen™ kit must have done something odd to her. Every time she

hiccups, a little flame
comes out of her beak . . .

and smoke
goes through
her nostrils.

2pm – Boris appointment with one-eared Clive, the vet.

One-eared Clive said he doesn't know what is wrong with Boris and that she is the oddest chicken he's ever met.

Boris pooed on his foot.

As we were leaving, MilDred came into the vet's with her parrot. She actually smiled at me!!

Don't *think* it was because her parrot threw up on me . . .

Only one more challenge to go. This will be my last chance to get the one hundred pounds for PARPS or my reputation and my ship will be gone

forever. And so far I've got zero points.
Just great.

My birthday!!! ☺ Spent today baking and
trying to stay out of everyone's way.

Boris laid another hexagonal polka-dot
egg in yellow – my favourite colour!

Lovely, until Redruth's birthday card
cannonball shot in through the porthole. ☹
Scrambled egg for tea.

Mum gave me her copy of *Proper
Pirating for Beginners*, written by my
Grandpa Greybeard before he died. She
says it might stop me performing worse

than a legless octopus. ☹

And Blackbeard? Blackbeard gave me
another letter from PARPS. ☹

I was baking my birthday cake when
he turned up. He thought my flowery
apron was "stupidly ridiculously rubbish"
and took photos to send to *Pirate Life*.
Sigh.

Here's the letter . . .

Pirates **A**gainst **R**ubbish **P**iracy **S**ociety

The Best Pirate Ship in the World

Dead Man's Cove

The Ocean

August 19th

Dear Barnacles Blunderbeard,

It has come to the attention of PARPS that you're bringing FURTHER disgrace to the name of pirate.

Recent reports include:

- Falling off a plank. *Falling!*

- Causing the destruction of thirty-eight ships belonging to fellow pirates, including one with a year's supply of my favourite Jackson's Jelly (made from real jellyfish).

- STILL failing to credit the YoHo Bank with any money WHATSOEVER.

- Having jelly beans for teeth (I mean, seriously, what is the matter with you??!!).

We hope you understand how serious this is and regret to inform you that, unless you do indeed wish to lose your ship and your career as a pirate, you must now fulfil the following even *harsher* conditions:

- Credit the YoHo Bank with one thousand pounds by the end of the year (nine hundred pounds more than previously requested).

- Pay PARPS one thousand pounds in compensation (to cover admin costs, time spent in meetings moaning about how rubbish you are, fish and chips and

ice cream required at said meetings,
etc., etc.). Before the end of the year,
please send us a cheque (payable to
Blackbeard) and a dozen of those
toffee cupcakes with swirly bits.

Yours absolutely, really furiously,

Blasterous Blackbeard

(Director of PARPS)

P.S. This is absolutely your last chance or
we'll take your ship and leave you on a

desert island with just your stupid
chicken for company.

FOR THE REST OF YOUR LIFE.

P.P.S. Mum's seriously not impressed
either and says she's stopping your
pocket money.

Well, that's it, then. How can I possibly
get out of this one? Even if I won the
POTY Award, that's only a hundred
pounds. Where on earth will I get the rest
of the money?

Started to pack for desert island. Wonder how many T-shirts I need?

Was slumped in my deckchair, nibbling a strawberry cupcake and feeling sad that my pirate career has to end this way.

I could have been brilliant – or at least a bit less rubbish. Then Boris flapped up on to my lap and looked at me. It's like she was my friend and wanted to help . . .

I decided that maybe Boris wasn't that bad after all.

Then she hiccupped and set fire to my trousers.

Trying to cheer myself up. Thought I'd invent a treasure-hunting device for the final POTY event on the Island of Death.

Everything I come up with is stupid.

Model 1: ChickenSkater™

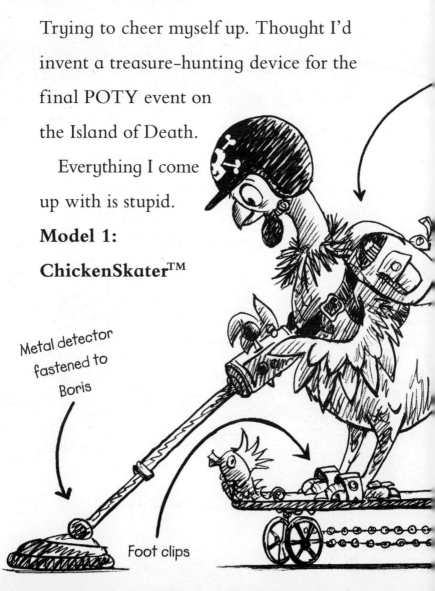

Metal detector fastened to Boris

Foot clips

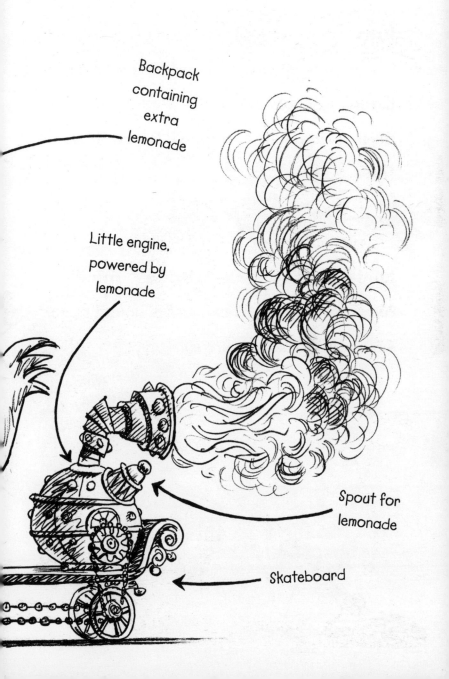

Backpack
containing
extra
lemonade

Little engine,
powered by
lemonade

Spout for
lemonade

Skateboard

Pros

Could speed up treasure hunt. Easy to make.

Cons

Boris + lemonade = AAAARRGHHHH!

SEPTEMBER 20TH

Model 2: The Peek-A-Brain™ mind-reading device (Blackbeard is bound to guess where the treasure is).

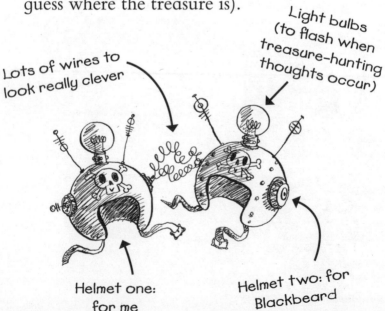

Light bulbs (to flash when treasure-hunting thoughts occur)

Lots of wires to look really clever

Helmet one: for me

Helmet two: for Blackbeard

Automatic pencil, paper and clipboard to write down thoughts

Pros

Er . . .

Come back to this bit later.

Cons

Getting Blackbeard to agree to wear it.

Getting Blackbeard to give away thoughts.

Getting it to work generally.

Fine! Forget it!!

OCTOBER 2ND

Here we go . . .

Dear POTY participant,

Congratulations on surviving so far. To have reached the third and final task of the competition, you can consider yourself worthy of the title "Pirate" (unless you are Barnacles Blunderbeard, in which case you can consider yourself worthy of the title "idiot". If you're reading this, you're only allowed to continue the competition because we are all hoping you'll do something ridiculous, like fall into a massive pit while treasure-hunting and be stuck there forever).

Please find below details of the final event:

EVENT THREE
Treasure-hunt on the Island of Death: November 1st

Location: Island of Death

Directions: Halfway across the ocean then left a bit

Time: 9am

Please bring: Treasure-hunting materials e.g. map, big spade, Satnav, etc.

Captain Harry Chomp

OCTOBER 17TH

Model 3: The Blaster-Hunter™

(my last hope).

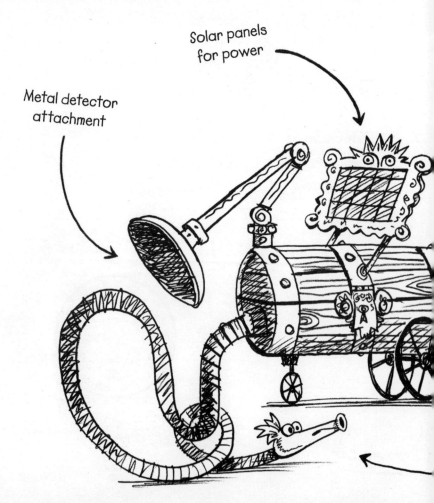

Solar panels
for power

Metal detector
attachment

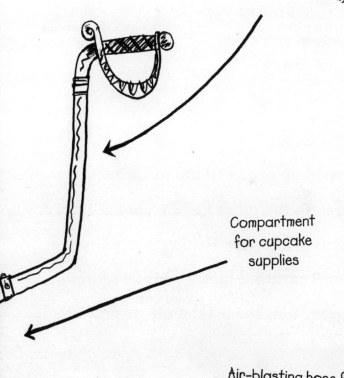

Mum's old vacuum cleaner, which I told her I'd take to Pirate Claire's Repairs (shhhh!)

Compartment for cupcake supplies

Air-blasting hose for blowing away sand (quicker and less effort than digging)

NOVEMBER 1ST

Event Three - Treasure-hunting: November 1st.
Up to ten points awarded for
technique. Another ten points to the
one who finds the treasure first.

What a day!

Turned up at the Island of Death
along with the other POTY contestants:
Captain Slasher the Rather Scary, Barber
Rossa, Redruth, Hooksy, MilDred and,
of course, Blackbeard the oh-so-perfect
pirate.

I was so nervous. It didn't help that
Blackbeard and Redruth kept grinning at

me, saying they had a nice treat in store for me. Nice? Those two? About as nice as a stingray in your bed.

Found the "treat".

It was this:

Yes, I'm ashamed to say I fell for Blackbeard's nasty little trick. I ran over to look at the sign, Boris tucked under one arm and the Blaster-Hunter™ tucked under the other. Suddenly the twigs and leaves disappeared under me and I ended up in a massive pit so deep there was no way I could climb out. And there was a cannonball in the pit.

Wrapped in pink paper.

Unwrapped it and read the note.

Dear Blunderbeard,

This should keep you out of the way
so us proper pirates can get on with
some treasure-hunting. You really are as
hopeless as your stupid chicken.

Your career as pirate is now officially
over. Hahahahaha!

See you at the POTY Award ceremony
when I win it again. Oh. Wait. No I won't.
You'll be stuck here!

Hahahahaha (in case you missed it the
first time).

Blasterous Blackbeard

(Director of PARPS)

Bad luck, Blunders! And ignore
Blackbeard. I'M going to win the POTY
Award with Dad as a judge!

R xxx

Of course Blackbeard was right. No money for the YoHo bank. No chance of claiming the POTY title, not that I ever had a chance. No hope of proving myself to Mum and my rotten brother. I was a total failure, stuck in a pit with a loopy chicken and a slightly odd-looking vacuum cleaner.

Then something amazing happened.

Boris went wild (nope, no lemonade involved). She suddenly squawked and started digging at a rate of knots. With Boris scrabbling wildly and me using the Blaster-Hunter™, we created a tunnel leading away from the pit. I was so puzzled – what was Boris doing?

Where was she taking us?

Half an hour later, I found out! We discovered a treasure chest.

Boris pecked at it like a hyperactive woodpecker until the lid was in tatters.

Then she hopped in and did this!

Turns out, she has a bit of a thing about gold – and she can smell it! Never knew that before – well, never had any gold on board my ship to find out!

I looked carefully at the stash of gold – coins with a dragon's head on one side. It was Captain Loozer's long-lost treasure hoard! The one stolen from Flametongue's cave!

I used the Blaster-Hunter™ to blast our way through the sand until we popped out right at the award ceremony.

Of course, Blackbeard had found the POTY treasure first and was about to be crowned the winner of the POTY Award.

(Redruth was furious. Her face was as red as her hair!)

My knees were shaking as I cleared my throat and declared to the judges that we'd found the lost hoard of Captain Loozer. I told them about Boris's amazing gold-detecting skills. She was surely the best pet a pirate could hope for. And I showed them my amazing Blaster-Hunter™, which helped us get to the gold quickly.

The judges were speechless (even Uncle Redbeard) and Blackbeard's face was a picture. (Several pictures, actually. Planning to frame these and put them up in my toilet):

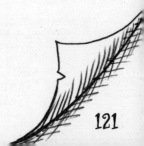

Then I heard the words – the words I thought I would never hear: "Pirate Blunderbeard, the judges have decided that YOU have won the Pirate of the Year Award!"

This is what the leader board looked like!

Blunderbeard: 100
Blackbeard: 50
Redruth: 45
Captain Slasher the Rather Scary: 41
Barber Rossa: 38
MilDred: 37
Hooksy: 31

The judges were so impressed (well, apart from Uncle Redbeard) that they awarded me one hundred points!

Uncle Redbeard just looked like he was going to explode.

Mum was so excited her false teeth shot out and latched on to Blackbeard's bum.

But, just as they were about to give me the Skull and Crossbones trophy, Blackbeard gave me an evil grin. He grabbed the biggest fish from Codd's Mobile Fish Van.

"Really?" he screeched hysterically. "You want to give this loser the POTY Award when he passes out at the sight of fish? Look!" And he ran towards me.

It was a horrible fish – all eyes and gaping mouth. My legs turned to jelly.

But then, when he nearly reached me, Boris stepped into his path. He tripped over her, sending the huge fish flying up into the air. Blackbeard fell flat on his back at my feet. Boris gave an enormous

hiccup and a flame flew out of her
mouth (she's not been the same since the
lemonade). Blackbeard could only watch
in horror as the flame passed over the fish

and a huge smoked salmon landed with a THUD on his face. Even MilDred was laughing.

I think, after today, fish are definitely
my friends, not my enemies! ☺

NOVEMBER 3RD

The judge who worked at the YoHo Bank
valued the stash.

It's worth one hundred thousand
pounds!!!!!!!!!!!!

Blackbeard actually *cried*.

I'd beaten Blackbeard! I had enough
money to pay one thousand pounds into
the YoHo Bank, one thousand to PARPS
and oodles left over!

I was saved!

NOVEMBER 17TH

Had photos of Blackbeard from the
POTY Award ceremony printed, and
hung them up in my toilet. Now I laugh
so much whenever I go into the bathroom
that I don't even think about piranhas
being in my loo.

Decided to use the cash to make loads
of new and fabulous inventions.

DECEMBER 9TH

Popped into Pirate Pete's Pets to buy Boris
a Chick-O-Snack Christmas pudding.

Asked Pirate Pete, out of curiosity,

where he'd got Boris from. He said he couldn't remember but he'd look it up if I made him a rather lovely gooseberry-cream cupcake. Deal.

DECEMBER 25TH

Merry Christmas! Lovely lunch with Mum on the *Golden Squid*. I even played with her pet catfish. Fish really aren't so bad after all.

Blackbeard was there too, moaning about being fired from PARPS. Mum made him wash up while she and I ate cupcakes.

Fortunately, I'd given Mum my

Scrub-O-Matic™ washing-up invention for Christmas.

Unfortunately, for Blackbeard, there are a few technical issues I forgot to tell him about ...

And this came from Pirate Pete:

Dear Blunderbeard,

Found these buried in the
paperwork from the bloke
who sold Boris to me. I never
look at paperwork. Might do
from now on.

Merry Christmas!

Pirate Pete

P.S. Please can I put in an order
for a Blaster-Hunter™?

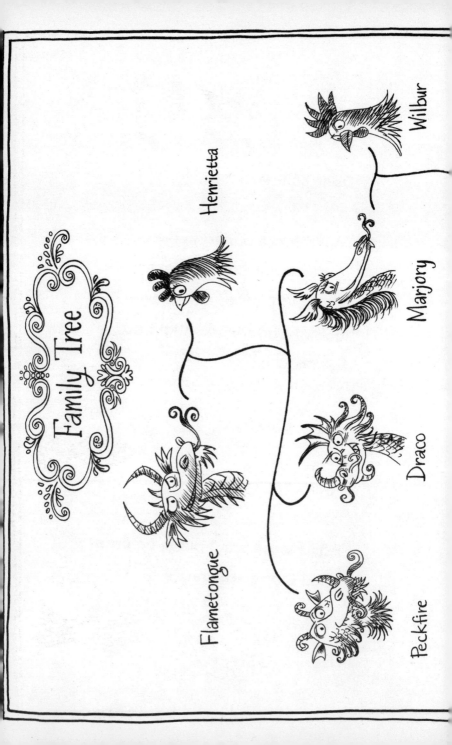

Family Tree

Henrietta

Wilbur

Flametongue

Marjory

Draco

Peckfire

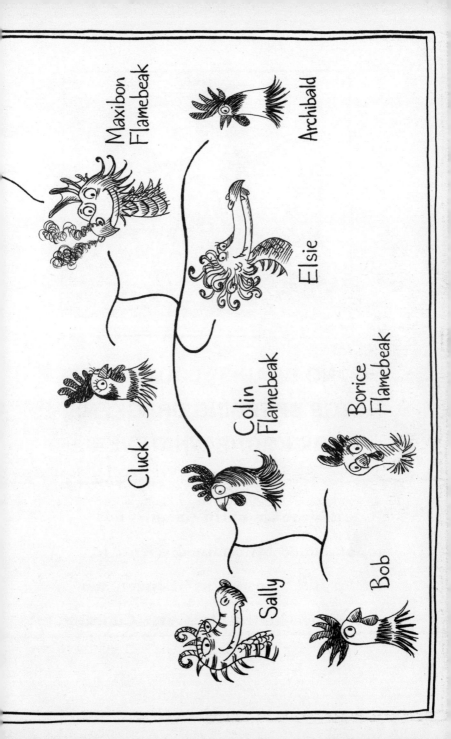

"NO BRAINS" LOOZER TO STOP BREEDING DRAGKENS/ CHICKGONS/WHATEVER!

A quite frankly nutty scientist has today ended his doomed scientific study. Bill "No Brains" Loozer, son of treasure-hoard-discoverer Captain

William Loozer, has officially brought a halt to his "interesting" experiment of breeding dragons and chickens.

"I'm a little bit disappointed really," said Bill. "I was so excited when Dad first came home with a dragon. I thought maybe we could get golden eggs. And they'd be really valuable. But I only ended up with one hexagonal, polka-dot egg and a lot of really weird chickens."

The scaly chest . . . the flaming beak . . . the hoarding of my brass buttons . . . loving the scent of gold . . . All makes perfect sense for a chicken with a bit of dragon-blood!

Boris/Borice is the best (mostly) chicken in the world.

DECEMBER 31ST

Done fairly well with my resolutions this year.

New Year's resolutions for tomorrow:

1. ~~Stop biting nails.~~ Still too hard.

2. Plan another treasure-hunting expedition with Boris.

3. Use remaining money to set up Blunderbeard's WonderWeird Contraptions and invest in Blaster-Hunter™ production – orders are flooding in from lazy pirates!

4. Get a pet goldfish.

5. Employ depressed Blackbeard – as toilet-cleaner? (Note to self: order piranhas from Pirate Pete.)

6. Stuff traditional pirating. Become the bestest cupcake-baking, gadget-inventing pirate on the seas EVER.

Pirate Blunderbeard and Boris will soon be setting sail on another adventure . . .

WORST. HOLIDAY. EVER.

My stupid brother has tricked me into the worst holiday ever . . . on the Island of No Return. I'm stuck here unless I can find a secret stash of treasure, in which case Blackbeard says he will come and get me (how nice of him). All I have to do is follow this treasure map through a jungle full of pirate-eating creatures (no problem), into the deepest, darkest, probably-haunted cave (not at all scary, not at all scary, not at all scary) and track down the hidden gold that is so well hidden everyone gets lost trying to find it (perfect). My life is ruined.

Pirate
Blunderbeard

And if they survive the Island of No Return

join Blunderbeard and Boris on the Worst.

Mission. Ever. . .

WORST. MISSION. EVER.

Sailing the seven seas with Grandpa
Greybeard sounded like a fun holiday,
even though we DID have to take my
annoying cousin Redruth. But it turns out
that Grandpa has a secret plan to capture
the ship of Dread Pirate Dreadlocks –
winner of the Scariest Pirate of the Year
Award. Easy peasy pants. What could
possibly go wrong . . . ?

Pirate
Blunderbeard